◄ Barti and Bel ►

WHIZZ
around
WALES

◄ Suzanne Carpenter ►

To the Higginses – my whizzy friends

Parents and teachers please note: all the sites featured here are suitable for a family visit, but at the National Library of Wales, Aberystwyth, while children are welcome in the exhibitions, shop and restaurant, they are not allowed in the reading rooms.

The author and publishers gratefully acknowledge the support of the **Wales Tourist Board**, in providing the majority of the background photographs for this book; thanks also for the photographic material provided by:
Cadw: Welsh Historic Monuments (Castell Coch and Beaumaris Castle)
The National Trust Photolibrary (© photograph of Penrhyn Castle)
National Library of Wales, Aberystwyth
Oakwood Park

First Impression – 2003

ISBN 1 84323 238 3

© illustrations and text: Suzanne Carpenter

This title is published with the financial support of the Welsh Books Council.

Printed in Wales at
Gomer Press, Llandysul, Ceredigion

Lots to see   Lots to tell

This is Barti   This is Bel

Hop, skip, jump, run

Follow us and have some fun

I like castles

I like moats

I like ships

I like boats

I like magic

I like towers

I like parks

I like flowers

I like rivers

I like lakes

I like cheese

I like cakes

I like beaches

I like waves

I like pirates

I like caves

I like mountains

I like hills

I like rides

I like thrills

I like kites

I like rooks

I like stories

I like books

I like farms

I like sheep

I like bed

I like sleep

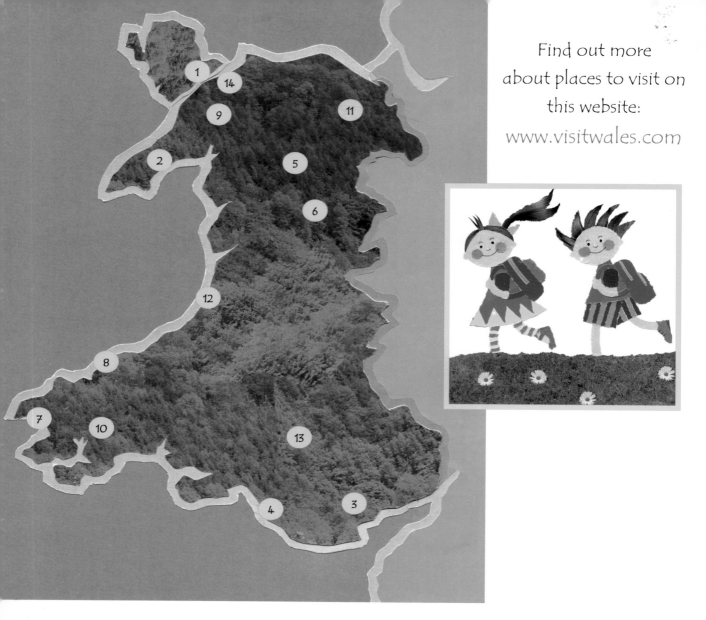

Find out more about places to visit on this website: www.visitwales.com

Where did Barti and Bel go?

1. Beaumaris Castle
2. Pwllheli
3. Castell Coch
4. Margam Park
5. Bala
6. Vyrnwy Lake
7. Newgale
8. Ceibwr
9. Snowdon Mountain Railway
10. Oakwood Park
11. Moel Famau
12. National Library of Wales
13. Brecon Beacons
14. Penrhyn Castle